Proscenium Street and Other Stories
Verlyn Flieger

Signum Press

Signum Press

ISBN (paperback): 978-1-959360-08-7
ISBN (ebook): 978-1-959360-09-4

Cover art and illustrations by Emily Austin
Illustration on page 18 by iStock.com / asmakar

Contents

To Vaughn Howland

Introduction

"The Otherworld is always right behind you," Verlyn Flieger writes in her poem, "Shelly at the Beach." But whether this observation should warn us or reassure us is far from certain. The stories in this collection present an eclectic range of literary styles, modes, and textures, but all of them meditate on the power of imaginative invention—our ability to create and understand fantasy in its myriad forms. What Tolkien calls "Faërie" or "the Perilous Realm," Professor Flieger describes in her scholarship as something "at once a literary construct, an imaginal exercise, a make-believe world, a place to go to, and an altered state of being—a series of ideas easier to picture than to explain."[1] This array of descriptions also captures the feelings created by the works found on the following pages—in which the boundary between what is real and what might be real is unpredictably flexible.

The title of both the collection and its opening story—"Proscenium Street"—alludes to this traversable boundary. This tale draws us into the collection just as its eminently sensible protagonist is drawn suddenly across a threshold, out of her day-to-day routine and into a surreal, existentially unmooring encounter. Whether the experience can be best understood as a dream or a hallucination—or whether, like Lucy passing through the wardrobe or Dante through the infernal gates, she has crossed into an entirely different realm—the story itself does not reveal. Rather, this reflection on identity and mortality illustrates how literary fiction helps us find meaning in our lived experience of reality.

Encountering the several forms of fantasy represented in this collection, characters are repeatedly forced to confront the point at which external reality ends and subjective experience begins. "A Waiter Made of Glass" dramatizes different responses to a single traumatic event, shaped by the limits of each character's powers of perception. In struggling to understand the experience, the characters are necessarily constrained by their imperfect knowledge of (or ability to understand) themselves. In "Gavál and Dórvos," two brothers wander in and out of each other's dreams just as they wander out of their own bodies into different corporeal forms. Perhaps the most traditional fantasy story, it resonates with works by the Brothers Grimm, Marie de France, and Philip Pullman, while also participating in the Romantic convention of the "found fragment." With the tale left deliberately incomplete, any further events that might continue this story must take shape in the minds of its readers.

Other stories, like "The Lion's Head" and "The Cap," together with "Saturday Night" and "Shadow and Sun," offer short parables about the potency of imaginative invention. Does an ostensibly magical cap really transform the appearance of its wearer? Could the drawing of a lion prove more alarmingly powerful than a real, living specimen? The answers to these and other questions illustrate the consequences of belief or disbelief in artistic creations—and in particular, the dangers of a kind of belligerent sensibility pushed to the extreme. Though each of these tales hints at a moral lesson without explicitly revealing it, none attempts to conceal or sheathe that lesson's sharp cutting edge. Rather, in tradition of the short stories of Roald Dahl, Flannery O'Connor, and Saki, each comes armed with a sting at the end.

The power of fantasy is clear even in stories that do not contain anything "fantastic"—or, at least, not according to the strict categorization of literary genres. "Dark Water Café" and "Outside" stand as fairy stories set entirely in our own mundane world. "Outside" shows us the most ordinary of settings through the perspective of a sheltered house cat—a creature thoroughly *of this world*, but who has seen very little *of this world*. Through her eyes, the story captures the alarming strangeness of objects and experience that, to most of us, would seem utterly unremarkable.

The events of "Dark Water Café" also take place within the strict boundaries of literary realism. While travelling in an unfamiliar city, the narrator's twilight wanderings take her down darkening streets, past buildings along a canal, and across a particular bridge. The account of what she finds there embodies the profound yearning, familiar to all readers of fantasy literature, for places and experiences beyond the reach of our ordinary lives. The story evokes C. S. Lewis's childhood memory of a marvelous toy garden. Though, in fact, simply the lid of a biscuit tin that his brother "had covered with moss and garnished with twigs and flowers," Lewis recalls the sudden longing that this miniature representation created in him: "What the real garden failed to do, the toy garden did."[2] For Lewis, the imperfect suggestion of an inaccessible something inspired a deeper reaction than the actual thing itself. So too, in this story, the narrator's disappointment at the offerings of a finite reality illuminates the emotional force of the unreal possibilities we imagine.

"Tall Grass," a dramatic monologue in prose, revisits this same sense of disappointment at life's shortcomings, but this time much more aggressively. Detailing a young run-away's journey across a prairie, the story's stylized language sharply contrasts the grim horrors of the plot—a series of violent events, both cruelly outlandish and depressingly possible. The most elemental materials of fantasy literature (the forced flight from one's childhood home; travel through a wide world fraught with dangers; the forging of unexpected friendships; and the confrontation of fierce enemies) all carry quite a different meaning for the narrator of this story than for the heroes of most fairytales, ancient or modern. Tolkien famously commended fairy stories for offering readers "Escape," not merely from the banal "noise, stench, [and] ruthlessness" of modern living, but also from "things more grim," such as "hunger, thirst, poverty, pain, sorrow, injustice, death."[3] This tale shows both the inadequacy and the necessity of narrative story-telling in circumstances where it may, in fact, be the only available means of escape.

Between light and language, life and loss, the mundane and the fantastical, this collection compels us to consider the interplay between what we know of this world and what we imagine of the Otherworlds that, as we are never allowed to forget, are "always just behind us."

— Dr. Liam Thomas Daley, University of Maryland (2025)

---

1. Verlyn Flieger, *Green Suns and Faërie: Essays on Tolkien* (The Kent State University Press, 2012), 67.

2. C.S. Lewis, *Surprised by Joy: The Shape of My Early Life* (Book-of-the-Month Club, 1997), 7.

3. J. R. R. Tolkien, "On Fairy-Stories," in *The Monsters and the Critics and Other Essays*, ed. Christopher Tolkien (London: Harper Collins Publishers, 2006), 151.

Author's Preface

I'm grateful to Signum Press for the opportunity to bring out a second edition of my collected short stories, and more than grateful to my editor Amy Troolin for her patience and encouragement during the process.

This new volume differs from the first in that it has no poems but offers five new stories to add to the original five. The new ones are "Proscenium Street," "The Cap," "Gavál and Dórvos," "Outside," and "Shadow and Sun." Put together, old and new add up to a round ten, a decade, a dectet, a tenner, a dozen minus two. No theme unites them; they are more of a heap than a sheaf, but the additions are an update on what I've been doing for the past year or so. I hope you like them.

As I explained in the first edition, it's a funny business, writing. You never know when the urge will hit or how the words will flow, let alone what they will turn into. The opening sentence of "Tall Grass" floated into my head on the road from Cheyenne to Laramie, and the rest took shape naturally. "Dark Water Café" grew out of an evening walk that crossed a bridge over the C & O Canal in Washington, D.C. A sidewalk table and two empty chairs inspired "A Waiter Made of Glass," while "Saturday Night" arose out of the insistent barking of some neighborhood puppies. "The Lion's Head" was a drawing by my five-year-old daughter that for fun we scotch-taped to the dining-room chandelier. It stayed there for years.

This has been equally true of the second edition. "Proscenium Street" started with the image of a woman stepping on a banana peel but sliding unexpectedly into a totally unforeseen otherworld. "Shadow and Sun" was inspired by the daily news. "Outside" resulted from my brief stint as a cat-sitter for my vacationing older son and his family. As for "Gavál and Dórvos," I don't know where it/they came from, except the dark side of my imagination. Now they are ready for yours. Whatever their genesis, their unresolved fate is now in the hands of you, the reader. Do with them what you will.

Good luck,

Verlyn

Proscenium Street

Julia

Julia Wentworth shrugged into her cardigan, slipped the grocery list into her pocket, clipped the leash onto her dog Rowdy's collar, and followed him out the front door. She was on her way to the greengrocer's, the butcher's, the baker's, and the vintner's in that order. Her plan—for Julia's life was always planned—was to select a bunch of the new asparagus just coming into season, to confer with the butcher about a veal chop for herself and a knuckle bone for Rowdy, to get some sweet rolls from the baker for tomorrow's breakfast, and to choose a bottle of red wine to go with the veal and asparagus for her dinner that evening.

Julia always accomplished what she set out to do, so it never occurred to her that she might not achieve these modest goals. Nor did it enter her mind that she might not come back from her errands, still less that she would find herself in a place so removed from where she expected to be as to seem more an Otherworld than a place one might visit, even by accident. Before the day was over all of these things would—or would not—happen. Not all at once but one after another after another.

The puppy was straining at his leash as she shut the door behind her. "All right Rowdy," she said, "lead the way." But she didn't mean it. Julia was a woman who liked things to be organized—her shopping, her day, her life—and Rowdy, even on a leash, had a way of running roughshod over her carefully laid plans for any or all of these. Rowdy was a bit of flotsam that had washed up on her doorstep one morning, damp and dirty and disheveled and in desperate need of salvage. His backstory was easy to read in the periodic convulsive shudder of his skinny body, the tucked-under tail glued to his belly, and the beseeching tenor of his glance. When she picked him up, he reached a tentative tongue to give her chin a lick, but his anxious brown eyes were searching hers to ask if that was all right? She told him of course it was, gathered him indoors, set him a bowl of leftovers to gobble, brushed the mud out of his scruffy, matted coat—tan with a darker brown patch on his back—and took him to the vet. The vet gave him a shot against distemper, a bath from which he emerged smelling of pine essence, and a guess that he was a mix of terrier and spaniel.

It may have been this odd genetic match that gave him his equally oddly matched ears—one perked for news, one at half-droop, thinking it over—and his rakish and enquiring air. It was the ears that inspired Julia to name him Rowdy, a name that fit both his investigative nature and his emerging personality. Rowdy's once-guarded eyes now took in every new sight that came his way. Rowdy's once under-tucked tail, no longer between his legs but flying behind him like a pennant, never missed a wag at any hand that might hold out a treat. Rowdy's exquisitely tuned nose now twitched at the first whiff of an interesting bouquet, and his leg never failed to lift as he passed a fire-hydrant or a lamp post.

Unlike the pup, his mistress ignored distractions, and this morning Julia was focused on her shopping expedition. It was a fine day, the sky bright and blue after an early shower, and as she walked along she breathed in the mingled smells of wet pavement, spring flowers, and budding trees that filled the air with fragrance. Except at the turning that led down to the river.

There the air was redolent with fragrance of an earthier sort, a whiff and more than a whiff of humanity in the raw, of un-washed bodies and un-attended trash and un-collected garbage all ripening in the sun. A few of the shops that fronted the street on both sides were open for business, but many were simply the temporary shelters of people with no place else to go.

No signpost marked the street, but it was spanned by an arch slung between two buildings that framed the short perspective and announced

PROSCENIUM STREET

in letters whose once ornate red and gold paint was now cracked and peeling. Proscenium Street was only two blocks long, a winding squiggle that ran from the town square down the hill to where the Old Theatre backed up to the river. No one in the upper part of town bothered to recall that the street's arch had once been meant to advertise the actual proscenium arch in the theatre at the bottom of the street. Legend said it had been there since the early days, when the first players strolled into town wheeling a cart loaded with props and costumes that doubled as a stage, and as nobody now living was old enough to contradict this, the story, like the street, persisted.

That theatre was now dark, the final bows taken, the play dissolved into thin air like the testimony of the actors, like the faded scent of greasepaint and powder, like the echo of applause. Like the dream as it fades when you first wake up.

'Where does the play go?' wondered Julia, 'when the performance ends?' 'There ought to be a place,' she decided, 'for a play to exist between performances, a sort of insubstantial green room where it waits for its cue to come to life once more.' The notion tickled her fancy, and she played with the idea like a child with a soap bubble. Rowdy, in contrast, was looking forward to the never-fading, ever-invading smells of Proscenium Street and tugged at his leash as they passed it by.

Julia felt a sneaking envy for the puppy's ability to get the most out of new experience, however odoriferous. 'But you are not a puppy,' she lectured herself sternly. 'You are a grey-haired old lady, a leftover, a relict, and you'd better start getting used to it. You have nothing to look forward to. No children, no grandchildren, and the man you loved is gone. Your life is behind you now, not ahead. It's all over.' A phrase drifted into her mind: 'There's no there there.' 'Well,' she answered herself, 'there's no here here either. It's all gone. There's nothing to discover, nothing new.' She shrugged again. 'I guess I'm just bored.'

In fact she was not so much bored as lonely, though she would never have acknowledged that. If anyone had asked her, she would have said she was just fine thank you, which was her stock answer to all enquiries of that kind. But every now and again, at the corner of Proscenium Street she would hesitate and gaze under the arch down its colorful, disorderly length, survey the unruly crowd that teemed along its sidewalks, and wonder what if? and think maybe. Then she would shrug and pass on by, much to Rowdy's chagrin.

"Morning, Ms. Wentworth." The postman, his leather bag dragging down one shoulder. "Lovely day."

"Good morning, Mr. Martin. Yes, isn't it? A beautiful morning. I'm glad the rain has stopped."

'He never complains,' she thought, 'even though most of the paper in that bulky old bag is utter rubbish. Advertising circulars, direct mail solicitations. Nothing but empty promises. Like me.'

"Out early, aren't you? Getting the jump on the day?"

"Trying to. But I'm not in charge, as you can see."

She gestured to Rowdy, who took the lift of her hand as his signal to make a sudden sprint and sharp turn that dragged her after him under the painted arch and onto Proscenium Street. They passed the fruit stand on the corner just under the arch, and a few steps later Julia's foot came down on something slick and slithery on the pavement. 'A banana peel,' she thought. 'How trite!' She barely had time for irritation at the careless eater who had dropped it when the discarded peel, speckled brown and half-decayed, skidded out from under her foot. Her leg went with it, the leash flew out of her hand, and she toppled backward, landing on her head. Rowdy kept on running.

The minute Julia's head hit the ground the banana-peel took off at warp speed and whizzed her down the length of Proscenium Street as on a toboggan, skidding her around curves, zipping her past storefronts, sending pedestrians diving in all directions, and finally crashing her to a halt bang up against the stage door of the theatre at the bottom of the street.

Davin and Rascal

"Hey Davin! Look what I found! A lady lying in the street! Wake up, lady!"

Everything was dark. She wasn't sure whether she was actually hearing the voice or if it was in her head. Her eyes were closed, and she thought her ears might be too.

"Are you asleep, lady?"

Of course I am not asleep, you silly git. I don't usually lie down in the middle of the street like a thrown-away candy-wrapper. I could be dead for all you know.

But the joke wasn't very funny, and there was no one to appreciate it but her. Or was there? She blinked her eyes into half-focus to see bending over her a dirty-faced little urchin of five or so, a raggedy, unwashed cherub in ill-fitting clothes.

"'m'not asleep," she mumbled. "Rowdy. Where's Rowdy?"

"Don't know Rowdy," said the cherub. "I'm Rascal."

A deeper voice that must be Davin chimed in. "Are you all right?"

The voice was coming from a great distance or maybe down a tunnel. Some place very far from everywhere.

"I'm just fine, thank you."

"You're sure?"

"Yes . . . I mean . . . no . . . I mean . . . I don't know."

"Do you know what happened?"

She shook her head, a bad mistake, as it made the world slide sideways.

"Can you stand? Let me help you." Hands gripped her shoulders—"Easy now . . . up you come!"—and raised her carefully to a standing position.

Her eyes were still blurry, and the world was spinning around her. She shook her head to clear it, but that made everything slide sideways again.

Davin's arms kept her from falling, and he said, "You'd better sit down."

She staggered a few wobbly steps and found herself perched on a wooden crate and gazing out from under the proscenium arch of the old theatre at the empty auditorium with its rows of vacant seats.

"Do you know where you are? Do you know who you are?"

She had to think about it, but finally said, "No. Neither one," and wondered to hear her own voice sound so strange.

"Did you hit your head?"

Her head still rocked like a rowboat in a storm. "I don't remember," she said. "I was going grocery shopping, but I stepped on a banana peel."

Her rescuer laughed. "How trite! That peel sure took you for a ride if it brought you all the way down here."

She meant to say "Where am I?" but she was still woozy, and it came out "Where am here?"

Davin didn't seem to think that odd. "Here is wherever you are whenever you are," he told her, as if it were too obvious to need explaining, "so you are always here."

The notion seemed so simple she was surprised that she had never thought of it before.

"But then . . . I don't mean to be rude, but . . . I have to ask . . . are you 'here'? I mean, are you real?"

"Certainly not," he assured her. "But then neither are you."

In her present state of mind Julia found this comforting. 'Then this is a dream,' she told herself, 'and I can wake up whenever I want.'

He heard her thought. "Oh no you can't. Least of all here."

"What's so special about here?"

"To start with, you're on Proscenium Street. Not only that, you're in a theatre. The proscenium—the arch that frames the stage where you're sitting—marks the interface between the play and the audience: that's to say, between dream and reality. You're in the middle of both, and that makes it hard to tell which is which."

Davin knew whereof he spoke. He was the last actor on Proscenium Street, the last relic of the theatre's former glory, and the right man to explain her new circumstances to Julia. With no job in prospect when the theatre closed, Davin simply stayed on after the others left, still playing the ghosts of his former roles no longer there yet still there. He sometimes wondered if he had simply become so absorbed into the parts he played that he had no presence without them. 'What happens to the role,' he asked himself, 'when the actor leaves it? Does it hang empty? Like a shirt without a wearer?'

The empty stage acted as Davin's bed-sitting-room, its old sets and props as his furniture, and he filled in the gaps with leftover fish-crates and discarded bottles washed up by the river. The bottles he fashioned into lamps, and the fish-crates were capable of infinite combination as tables, chairs, shelving, and cupboards. He followed the same practice with food, scavenging discards from dumpsters and trashcans, recombining his findings over a two-burner gas ring near the stage door. He did the washing-up in the backstage bathroom.

The other member of this improvised household was Rascal. Like the bottle-lamps and the fish-crate furniture Rascal was flotsam, one of the many buoyant discards washed up by the river. Curled into a floating trash can lid like a just-born pup, eyes still squeezed shut against the light, he had bumped up against the foot of Proscenium Street on the crest of a spring flood. Naked as a jaybird, he bore no indication of where he came from, and no one was around to claim him, so Davin scooped him out of the lid, brought him home, fed him, scrounged him some cast-off clothes, and coaxed him through his ABCs, a labor which comprised the beginning and end of his education. Proscenium Street was his finishing school.

For lack of a better name he called the foundling Trashcan, soon shortened to Rashcan and then to Rascal, where it stuck. The raucous, bustling street was Rascal's home, where he fitted comfortably into its spontaneous lifestyle. In the upper town people lived in houses and made appointments and paid calls in the afternoon. On Proscenium Street, camaraderie was of a different sort, life was lived in the moment, enjoyment seized on the wing. Folk staged street concerts with improvised instruments—tin buckets, galvanized washboards, and metal trash cans—or they held swimming races by torchlight or practiced line-dancing in the street. Spontaneous potluck parties might evolve along the storefronts, and if it rained, folk crowded into the theatre and onto the stage with Rascal running around underfoot and helping himself to Davin's cooking from everyone's plates. The theatre and its environs were all the world they needed.

Lady and L ᴬ ᴅ

"You need some quiet," said Davin. He held out a hand to Julia and gently, cautiously pulled her up standing. "Can you walk?" he asked, and she meant to say "yes," but it came out "yumph." Once she was steady on her feet, he steered her through the darkness of backstage to the half-open door of a dressing-room and pushed it wide.

Directly opposite the door was a vanity makeup table with a triptych mirror whose open wings re-reflected both the center panel and each other, all at slightly different degrees of slant. The effect was to put all the objects in all the mirrors in conversation with one another. This included Julia as well as a rack of costumes against one wall and a hat-stand in a corner that carried an assortment of wigs, everything from Rapunzel to Raggedy Ann to Cleopatra.

"Sit down," said Davin, easing her into the chair. "Make yourself comfortable."

That was not just ridiculous; it was out of the question. Comfortable was exactly what she wasn't. She had no idea who she was or where she was. She had run off a cliff and was scrabbling about over empty air like Wile E. Coyote in a cartoon chase. 'This isn't happening,' she told herself. 'Pretty soon I'll wake up and everything will be the same as it always was.' But she had a feeling that in this strange, hallucinatory world nothing would be the same as it always was. She felt like Alice in Wonderland. Like Dorothy in Oz. Like herself on Proscenium Street.

Rascal appeared at the door carrying a large, ragged square of brown cardboard torn from an old carton. He had found a red crayon somewhere and printed L ^{A} D in large straggly letters on the cardboard.

"It's your sign," he explained, "to remind you who you are."

"Thank you, Rascal," she said. She traced the letters with her finger. "It was kind of you to know I'd need something to help me remember. I guess L ^{A} D belongs on Proscenium Street."

Davin took the cardboard from her, squared it up it on the dressing-room door, stuck in a couple of thumbtacks, and stood back to admire the effect.

"Might have been made for you," he said. "Come to think of it, it was made for you. Find a wig to go with it, and your makeover will be complete." He pulled a wig at random off the stand. "Here," he said. It was the Raggedy Ann. She allowed Davin to settle the wig on her head, where the yarn curls fell in her eyes and made it hard to see where she was going. But that was all right because the one thing she knew was that though she was walking out the door, she didn't know where she was going.

She had barely exited the dressing-room when there came a frantic barking from stage left, and Rowdy hurled himself at her, knocking her off her feet. 'That makes twice he's done that,' she thought, as Rowdy planted all four paws on her chest and began straightaway to cover her face with slurping doggy kisses. He was tangled in his leash, which had wound itself around his legs.

You left me! accused his eyes. *I couldn't find you*, he complained. And with stern reproach: *Don't ever go away again.*

With what she felt was commendable tact she decided not to tell him it was the other way round, that what had happened was all his fault. Indeed, she felt like thanking him instead. Whatever had happened, however it had happened, whatever strange place she was now finding herself in, it was Rowdy who had brought her here, and she was grateful. In fact, she was just fine, thank you.

Rowdy seemed to be just fine as well. He had stopped licking her face, and waited patiently while she unwound the leash from around his legs, and wagged his tail, angling for a treat. She sat up and reached into her pocket for a puppy biscuit. With it came a piece of paper. She gave Rowdy the biscuit.

"What's that paper?" asked Rascal.

It took her a minute to remember. "It must be my grocery list from before . . . from this morning. I'd forgotten all about it."

She smoothed the crumpled paper as the words stared up at her.

Asparagus (bunch).

Veal Chop.

Knuckle Bone (Rowdy).

Sticky Buns.

Beaujolais nouveau.

"It looks like a poem," said Rascal. "Will you read it to me, Lady?"

"Yes," she said, and thought it odd that she didn't find it odd to be invited to recite her grocery list out loud to a complete stranger. The words looked so peculiar they might have been written in another language. Or another life. She started to read:

Asparagus a bunch for lunch
Veal chop for dinner meat
For Rowdy there's a knuckle bone
For me sweet buns complete
My journey down the winding way
That is Proscenium Street.

"That is not what I wrote," she declared, staring at the page with a frown. "I don't even know what it means."

"Maybe it means what it says," said Davin.

She didn't answer, just stared at Rowdy, and Rowdy stared back at her. His right ear flopped haphazardly, like a sail when the wind drops suddenly. Then his left ear came to attention like a soldier on duty. He stood up and stretched luxuriously, back legs fully extended, then front legs ditto. He lifted his head in the air, then lowered his nose to the ground and returned to the dressing-room door with the L ^{A} $_D$ sign. It had swung shut, but when Rowdy sat and scratched for entry, it opened by itself, just a crack but enough to release a narrow bar of light that fell across Julia's eyes.

"Come in," said her voice. "We've been waiting for you."

Julia Redux

But when she pushed the door wide and followed Rowdy in, there was no one in the room. The light was so clear it hurt, and all she saw was sharp as shattered crystal and as unreal as a stained-glass window. A trio of Julias stared out at her and sidelong at each other from the self-reflecting mirrors of the vanity, each of them with the Raggedy Ann wig tilted rakishly over one eyebrow.

The central mirror showed the woman who had started out to go shopping that morning. That woman stared at Julia so defiantly that she felt scorched by the suppressed anger. The frown lines that scored the forehead, the wrinkles that netted the face like a veil, scarcely masked the incandescent rage that burned below the surface. It was the rage, not the image, that took Julia by surprise. 'It's been there all along!' she reflected, 'and I didn't know. How very odd.'

The right-hand mirror profiled the woman who had ridden the banana-peel under the arch, surprised and sick and dizzy and overwhelmed with shock and unexpected sensations. Her wig was knocked even further askew, about to fall off. The woman in the left-hand mirror reached a hand to steady it as Julia also reached up to press it down on her head.

It was at that exact moment that all of the Julias merged, the ones in the mirrors and the one who saw them for the first time, the Julia who was and was not the woman who had set out to go grocery-shopping that morning.

It was at that exact moment too that Rascal's high-pitched little boy's voice came floating through the darkened theatre like a scarf in an updraft.

"Lady! Where are you, Lady?"

"Here," she called.

She remembered her own voice saying "Where is here?" and she started to answer herself.

"*Here* is wherever. . ." and then she stopped, afraid to repeat the slogan in case it might not work the second time around, in case the elliptical, interlocking, double-lobed rhythm that fit so smoothly with the pulse of this other world would lose the beat and she would be wakened out of her dream.

The dressing-room door banged open, and in came Rowdy and Davin and Rascal, as innocent and unconscious a trio of the three fates as ever haunted any life.

Julia was still clutching the piece of paper, now scrunched and dog-eared, that she had put in her pocket so long ago that morning.

"That's your poem," said Rascal. "I liked it. Will you read it one more time?"

"Happy to oblige," said Julia. She began to read.

Asparagus (bunch).

Veal Chop.

Knuckle Bone (Rowdy).

Sticky Buns.

Beaujolais nouveau.

"Not like that," said Rascal. "That's not how you read it before. Read it the right way."

"Okay," she said.

Asparagus a bunch for lunch
Veal chop for dinner meat
For Rowdy there's a knuckle bone
For me sweet buns complete
My journey down the winding way
That is Proscenium Street.

"All that about eating makes me hungry," said Rascal, rubbing his midsection. "My tummy keeps yelling that I haven't eaten anything since breakfast."

"And what did you eat for breakfast?" asked Julia. She didn't really care what he had eaten for breakfast, but the longer she could keep them both talking the longer she could stay in the dream.

"Nothing special," said Rascal. "Just the banana I stole from the fruit stand on the corner by the arch."

Lion's Head

W hen she was three years old, Ellen drew a picture of a lion's head on construction paper with an orange crayon and cut it out—all jagged around the mane—with her round-edged scissors.

"It's wonderful, darling," said her mother. "We'll put it up for Daddy to see when he comes home."

So Ellen got the Scotch tape and stuck a piece on the lion's head.

"Where do you want it, honey?" asked her mother. "On the door of your room? The refrigerator?"

"On the dining room chandelier," said Ellen.

So, though she thought it an odd place for a picture, let alone a lion's head, her mother reached up and stuck it on an arm of the dining room chandelier.

When Ellen's father came home that night, he admired the picture extravagantly and declared that he had never seen a better picture of a lion's head. "Looks just like a real one," he told Ellen. "I like the mane."

Her brother made fun of it, as brothers will, and was told he couldn't do any better when he was three so be quiet.

After a while, it was just one more thing hardly noticed, like the pictures on the wall.

A few weeks later, Ellen's mother, dusting the room for cobwebs, brushed the picture with her duster and reached up to take it down and put it away. Then she stopped her hand. No. That would hurt Ellen's feelings; she was so proud of it.

So the picture stayed where it was.

In time, it became a fixture there on the chandelier, always seen, never noticed, invisible in its familiarity. Once in a while, a dinner guest would make a comment or ask a question and be told that it was Ellen's lion. Ellen began to be embarrassed about it. She grew steadily older than three and thought the picture was childish.

"Mom, I think we should take that old thing down; it's been there for ages, and it looks silly."

"What looks silly?" asked her mother, not looking.

"The lion's head. You know, product of my short-lived artistic talent."

Her mother looked up, looked back to that three-year-old child, looked at the chandelier.

"Let's keep it. It's been there so long I think if we moved it now the chandelier would fall down."

So it stayed where it was.

Ellen grew older. Friends became boyfriends. From an embarrassment, the lion's head became a conversation piece: a way to break the ice if dinner got too awkward.

"I think it's awful," Ellen would say, "but it's been there for centuries. Mother treasures it because I drew it when I was three. She thinks if we took it down now the chandelier would fall down. And I wouldn't want to risk it. You never know. She might be right."

By now it was family folklore, and everyone played along that the lion's head was holding up the house. They made it a joke to reassure themselves that it was ridiculous: protection from the little coiled snake of fear we have deep inside that tells us we might need protection.

One day, Ellen brought a young man home with her from college to spend Thanksgiving with the family. He was a year ahead of Ellen in school and very much aware of it. It soon became clear that Ellen was aware of it, too, and anxious that the family should take him at her value.

At the end of Thanksgiving dinner, they were lingering over their pumpkin pie and coffee, all a little too full, as is only right at Thanksgiving, when the young man noticed the lion's head.

"Whatever is that?" he asked, looking quizzically at Ellen.

"That's our totem," said Ellen, smiling at him. "I made it when I was three, and it's been there on the chandelier ever since. We don't dare take it down for fear the chandelier will fall."

If she had said "*might* fall" or "we pretend the chandelier will fall," he could have let it pass. But he knew a challenge when he heard one.

"You're not serious. You don't really believe that."

Ellen also knew a challenge when she heard one.

"I am serious and I do believe it." She realized quite suddenly that she meant what she said. He could at least play along. "I mean it. If anyone took that lion's head off the chandelier, it would fall down."

He smiled at that and glanced around the table for answering smiles. Getting none, he smiled harder. "I dare you to take it off."

"No way," said Ellen.

"Do you dare me to take it off?"

"No way," said Ellen.

"Then I dare myself."

He stood up from his chair, reached out and up to the chandelier, and tore off the lion's head.

"I'll put it back," he told them all. "I just wanted to show you."

He smiled down at everyone, the lion's head gripped in his thumb and forefinger. A slight tremor shook the room, and the chandelier began to sway.

He was still smiling as the lights flickered and went out and plaster dust sifted down from the crack that opened in the ceiling. Then the ceiling sagged and buckled, and in the next moment the chandelier fell crashing onto the table, smashing the coffee cups and dessert plates and embedding itself in what was left of the pie. Ellen's family stayed sitting around the table. No one moved. No one got up. No one made a sound.

The Cap

I 'm back at home now, and having second thoughts; wishing I'd never laid eyes on the wretched thing, let alone agreed to that absurd price. I write "absurd" because the only way I can address the whole affair is to treat it as a joke.

Well, that's what Carnival is all about isn't it? An occasion for practical jokes, the broader the better? A license to misbehave? A time to cut loose and try something different?

In the first place—but is there ever a true "first" place? Something with nothing that came before it? Permit me to doubt.

Sorry, I digress. Try again.

The first place was The Costume Shop. Normally I avoid such frippery like the plague. But the approach of Carnival had challenged my hidden desire to escape my humdrum self. I wasn't the only one, of course, not in a store whose only merchandise is pretense. Yet I felt curiously isolated. Ignored by salespeople, jostled by customers, I stood in the middle of the aisle feeling both detached and overwhelmed by all the commotion going on around me.

Plain girls were turning themselves into princesses; snub-nosed boys transformed into knights or tin soldiers; vulnerable children become lions or tigers. One small boy was swallowed up in a green dragon twice his size. He defied his mother's order to take it off, and blundered around the shop gleefully bumping into people.

A pretty girl tried on a rhinestone tiara too big for her. It kept slipping over one eye, but she just kept admiring herself in the mirror. When she noticed me staring, she turned away. But she kept her grip on the tiara.

I, on the other hand, was losing my grip on the whole idea. I had enough trouble being myself, let alone some fantastic avatar. To avoid looking as out of place as I felt, I made a little play of riffling through the hangars draped with other peoples' fantasies—wizards, fairies, clowns, witches, ogres, ghosts.

Yet when the clerk—a smarmy-looking type with the smile of a snake in the grass—finally approached me, I had nothing to buy. The feeling was mutual, for he had nothing to sell. At first.

After an awkward pause he said, "Looking for something in particular?"

By that time the only thing I wanted was the exit.

"Yes," I said, half in jest. "A flying carpet."

He was not amused. "That would be in Trance-Portation," he said smoothly, "but I believe they've sold the last one."

"Well then, how about a ring of invisibility?"

"Illusory Effects, second floor."

"I don't even want to be on the first floor," I told him. "I just want to get away."

"Ah," he said. "Why didn't you say so?"

He beckoned me over to a hat-rack full of fright-wigs in garish colors, their crude seams visible amid the pink and green polyester hairs.

I shook my head. "I said get 'away,' not 'attention.'"

His eyes narrowed. Without even turning around he reached up behind his head to a high shelf and pulled down a shabby little item of knitted wool like an Irish fisherman's cap.

A shower of dust came with it, making me sneeze.

"Bless you!" he said, and held the cap out to me with both hands. I should have known, right then.

"This should do it," he said.

Smart-ass. "Do what?"

"Get what you asked for. 'Not-attention.'"

"And what is 'not-attention'?"

"Inconspicuosity."

"There's no such word," I told him.

"There is now," he said, and went into his sales pitch. "Most people look without seeing," he explained. "The cap will collaborate with that. Wearing it, you'll be unnoticed, ignored, overlooked."

"I already have been," I said. "In this very shop this very day. Without the cap."

"But with the cap it will be on your terms. You'll be the proverbial fly on the wall."

He slid his fist inside the brim and waggled it suggestively. "See? Nobody there."

"Of course there's nobody there when no one's wearing the cap," I said. "What kind of fool do you take me for?"

He started to answer, but changed his mind. "Try it on," he coaxed. "You'll see what I mean."

The cap didn't fit with the rest of the shop paraphernalia. But then, neither did I. I put it on.

I felt no immediate change, and was about to take it off when a frantic dad chasing a toddler ran bang into my shoulder, but he only stumbled, got his balance and ran on, muttering about loose floorboards.

The clerk steadied me against the counter. "See what I mean?" He smiled.

Aha! I thought. I get it. A way to participate without taking part. "I'll take it," I told the clerk.

It wasn't till he was wrapping it that I remembered to ask how much it cost.

"That's negotiable," he assured me. "This is the only one left, so I could let you have it for half-price."

"And what is half price?"

"A deal," he crooned. "A steal. Merely that I be there when you wear the cap."

"You don't want much, do you? If that's half price, what would be full price?"

"Your soul," he said. "But that too is negotiable."

Tuesday 8:00 a.m.

"Inconspicuosity" my foot. That was just sales-talk for snake oil, aka fraud. I know, because I put on the cap after breakfast—purely as a joke, you understand, to see what would happen—and got exactly what I suspected. Nothing. I am still plainly manifest, and the clerk has not come down the chimney.

As I wrote those words the doorbell rang.

Shall I confess? I opened the door in the hope that there would be something fantastic on the other side, though I wasn't sure what it would be. A wizard in a pointy hat? A fairy godmother with a wand? A green dragon twice my size?

There was no one. Not even an ordinary person. Just the empty street stretching away in both directions, not a soul in sight. A Carnival prankster, I thought, ringing doorbells and hiding. Or maybe just a short in the wiring. An electronic trickster.

I turned to go back into the house, but my way was blocked by a nondescript individual wearing a knitted woolen cap.

I didn't recognize him, but I heard his voice in mine and mine in his as each of us asked the other the only question that is ever worth asking.

"Who are you?"

A Waiter Made of Glass

Two men rendezvous at a sidewalk café on a street corner. The sign above the café door reads "Before & After." One man is already seated at a table on the bend of the corner. The second man arrives, pulls out a chair, and sits down. The first man is weathered, deep creases scoring his cheeks from nose to mouth. His eyes, wrinkled at the corners, are narrow against the light. The second man is younger, clear-eyed and fresh-faced, though his hands occasionally twitch, and his skin seems oddly grayed, as if seen through a dusty window. The two men look at each other, then away, then back. The younger man speaks first.

"Sorry to keep you waiting."

"Not a problem. The time seemed to pass."

"And here I am."

"Good to see you."

"The damn waiter didn't see me. Stared right through me. As if I wasn't there."

"I mean, it's good that you got here."

"Too right it is, seeing I very nearly didn't. I remember at one point wondering if I'd make it."

"A big 'if.'"

A pause. The younger man drums his fingers on the tabletop.

"It's funny, for a couple of minutes right at the end there—all the shooting—I thought for sure I'd bought it."

"Did you, now."

"Even sitting here, you know, I still can't believe . . ."

"Believe what?"

"That it's over."

"Too quiet?"

"Maybe. I'd like to see more . . ."

"Signs of life?"

"Signs of something. Anything. Everybody seems dead compared to . . ."

"Compared to us?"

"Yes. If you will have it. Compared to us."

"You can't not be changed, after something like that."

"No, no, I'm fine. It's the world that's changed." He looks away. "Everything looks transparent. Made of glass. That waiter—I can see right through him and out the other side."

"The same way he looked at you."

"I'm waving, but he's ignoring me. And you, too. You'd think these chairs were empty, the way he's staring right past us."

"Did you want to order?"

"Ah, he's seen me now and he's coming over. Damn. He's got customers with him. Those two women."

"They certainly don't seem dead. Or made of glass."

"I do not want to share this table."

"We may have no choice."

The waiter pulls out two chairs, speaks to the women: "Will this table do?"

The older woman smiles, nods. "Yes, this is perfect. Looking both ways."

She sits rather heavily, teetering the fragile chair. The younger woman, still standing, hesitates. "Are you sure we . . . ? I mean, wouldn't it be safer inside? We're pretty exposed here. This is the corner . . . "

"Nonsense. You know what they say about lightning not striking twice. Take a chair, my dear. He's waiting."

The waiter speaks: "Do you want a menu?"

The older woman shakes her head. "Just something to drink. A wine cooler, perhaps. With soda. Make it two."

The waiter leaves. The younger woman, now seated, hesitates again. "I don't really think I . . ."

"Don't be silly. A glass of wine will do you good. Keep your spirits up. Yes, yes, I know what you're thinking. It's a dreadful thing, of course. Dreadful. But that's just why we have to fly our colors. Show everybody we're still here. That's my view."

The waiter returns, sets down two tall glasses, ice tinkling, bubbles fizzing. "Anything else?"

The older woman speaks: "No, no, we're fine. Nothing more at the moment, thanks. But would you take away these empty chairs? They're obstructing the view."

Dark Water Café

The terrace of my hotel overlooked the canal, giving a view of unexceptional dreariness on the opposite bank: a dingy, brick-walled warehouse half concealed by a stand of willows. Despite the dullness of the vista, the terrace in summer was alive with people sitting in little white chairs at little white tables, chatting, gesturing, and sipping drinks. Then came autumn, and the winds swept the terrace clear. The willow leaves yellowed and fell in little showers of pale gold, and the brick wall was exposed in all its shabby utility. The tables and chairs were stacked away, as were the guests, who stayed inside to look from the tall windows of the hotel dining room on the bare trees and the dingy bricks of the warehouse.

An unusually fine November late summer—an unbroken series of high, clear days and mild air—called a few of the less retiring souls out to enjoy the terrace while they still could, to lean on the railing and watch the sun reflected in the dark, still water. I was one of these, and I found a perverse pleasure in thus prolonging my summer beyond its proper season. I stayed long hours staring at the few and yellow leaves that floated on the water's surface, feeling somehow that I maintained the good weather by the force of my presence above the water.

Late one afternoon, I was returning to the hotel from an expedition to the lower part of town. Though it lacked some hours yet to dinnertime, the early dusk of autumn was already closing in, and in the houses and shops the lights were coming on. Crossing the little bridge that spanned the canal, I paused to enjoy the reflection of all those lights in the water. It was then I noticed for the first time that the hotel had an under-story.

A lower terrace fronted the canal so immediately that the water lapped its edge. Tucked behind the terrace, I saw a little café whose lighted windows trembled on the water. They had the charm and magical appeal of those Easter eggs one had as a child, whose narrow end was fitted with a window that opened on a miniature scene alluring in its remoteness and inaccessibility. I was so enchanted by the vision that I stayed watching for some minutes, like someone at a play. Really, it was delightful: the still black water, the secret terrace with its lamps against the dark, the bright windows with their glimpse of hidden, delicious life behind them. But one could not stay looking forever, and at last I tore myself away and continued up the street.

That night at dinner—I dine alone, at a table by the window—I mentioned the café to my waiter and inquired how one found it from the hotel proper, for I could find no staircase that led down. He was quite bewildered at my question. A café? On the lower floor? But there is no lower floor. No, really; only the cellars and storerooms, dark and unwindowed. No, no, I assure you, nothing else. To my insistent questions (for the more he protested, the more I wanted that little café) he made polite replies, finally making his escape with an awkward laugh. Later, I saw him glancing sidelong at me as he whispered to a fellow waiter.

I thought some of exploring for myself when I had finished dinner. I began to have an idea where the stairs might be, for I retrieved a fugitive memory of seeing them, winding down and down. They were narrow and rather steep, like the stairs one descends in dreams. But then I thought the search would be better in daylight, and so instead passed the evening hours with a magazine and went early to bed.

The succeeding days were busy ones, and my affairs took me to the upper part of the town and farther, into the outlying districts. The terrace and the hidden café retreated to a corner of my mind. Not till a week later did I again find myself walking up the street, pausing as before on the bridge to enjoy the evening. The water was still and dark and gave no reflection of my head and shoulders as I leaned over. I was not thinking of the café, truly, when I saw the lights come on. The terrace glowed up at me from the water, and figures passed and passed behind the lighted windows. I suddenly wanted to go there, to join that life that seemed so much richer and fuller than my own, so much livelier than the quiet bridge, so much warmer than the chilly street.

It needed only a moment for me to perceive my mistake and to laugh with the waiter at my own absurdity. Of course there was no lower floor, no lighted terrace, no bright café. There was only the reflection in the dark water of the hotel I knew, the terrace I had sunned on, and the dining-room behind it where I had sat looking out the window. The whole illusion was simply the effect of light on the water, a trick of the view, no more: the deception of the eye compounded by the soul's longing.

I cannot tell you how bleak and empty it felt. I was bereft, robbed in an instant's awareness of a world I had longed so much to enter. It was worse than a prohibition, worse even than rejection. I could have borne "thou shalt not." I could not face "it was not." I left it then, the beckoning world that no longer existed, and went up to the hotel. I was not hungry for dinner, and I did not want to see the waiter. I retired early to bed, hoping a crossword puzzle would lead me to sleep.

I took care to avoid the bridge after that, but I could not forget the lost café. It made a sore place in my mind, a gap like a missing tooth that the insistent tongue revisits to explore.

Winter closed in; the nights came sooner; the night sky was lit with stars and the earth's darkness with the lights of the town. I knew the other lights would be there too, in the water, and I would not let myself look for them. But the more I fled the café, the more it pursued me. Constantly I saw in my mind's eye the lighted terrace, vacated just at that moment by the figures passing and re-passing now behind the windows. I heard their voices. I saw their life. I felt the warmth and waiting welcome of the phantom company.

I was so alone I could not bear it, and so at last one night I came to the bridge again and looked down into the water. Yes. It was there, hovering just at the edge of sight: a beckoning, secret world more real, more compelling than the one in which I stood, and as I looked I knew that I could go there, that it waited for me.

As I broke the water, the café blurred and wavered, and the lights went out.

Shadow and Sun

Two children played under the shadow of a wall that encircled the top of a hill like a wreath. Or a battlement.

One child said to the other, "Let us make a pretend that the shadowy part belongs to me and the sunny part beyond it belongs to you. The two are separate, and you cannot come onto my shadow unless I say."

The other child said, "They are not really separate; they just look different in different lights. The sunshiney part is farther from the wall, so I cannot reach it without crossing your shadow."

"Unless I say you can," said the first child. "That is the point."

"But we are friends," said the second child. "What you propose will divide us."

"No," said the first child. "It will define us. We will know for sure what belongs to each."

"But the shadow of the wall moves as the day passes," said the second child. "It keeps changing."

"We must follow as it moves," said the first child. "That is the game."

At that moment a cloud passed across the sun, casting another shadow on the hillside.

"Who does that belong to?" inquired the second child.

"It is shadow, so it's mine," said the first child.

"But it's in the middle of my sunshine," argued the second child. "So it's mine."

Neither of them thought the shadow belonged to the cloud.

"It's mine," said the first child.

"No, it's mine," said the second child.

The first child threw up both arms in a gesture that knocked the second child half across the line of division. The line was so sharp it seemed to cut the second child in half.

"I didn't mean to do that," cried the first child. "It was an accident. I'm sorry."

"It wasn't an accident!" said the second child. "And you're not sorry. You meant it. We are enemies now, and it's all your fault. You knocked me into the shadow, and now I will claim both shadow and sun as mine."

"Oh no you won't," said the first child.

"Oh yes I will!" said the second child, and hit a return blow that seemed to cut the first child in half.

And so it went on and on and on for a long while until a third child joined the game by claiming ownership of both shadow and sun, and when the other two protested, by knocking them both down one after the other. Both lay where they fell, each cut in half by sun or shadow but both so possessed by their own that they no longer knew one another, and so the third child won.

Who made the wall?

No one knew.

What was the fight about?

"Shadow," said one.

"Sun," said the other.

Who began it?

Each said the other.

No one cared.

Saturday Night

"The goddamn barkers are at it again tonight. I no sooner opened the door to get the paper than they started up. I swear to God, somebody ought to do something about them."

Geoffrey Fuller rattled the sports page.

"Who are the Barkers?"

His wife kept her eyes on the cucumber she was slicing for the salad. She had a fast right hand, which was rapidly turning the cucumber into a row of tidy little discs on the chopping board.

"The dogs, dummy. How dense can you get? The dogs next door."

"Well, you said 'The Barkers' like it was a couple. How did I know you meant dogs and not people? You said they were 'at it again.' Sounded like Saturday night in suburbia."

"Don't be cute. You know very well what I meant. What do you want me to call them? The American Kennel Club? 101 Dalmatians?"

"If you don't like the dogs barking," she said, "don't go out the door when they're in the yard. They're only puppies. The sight of you riles them for some reason."

She started in on a red pepper, her knife biting into the chopping board with more vigor than was really needed.

The newspaper rattled. "What's that you're making?"

"Salad."

"Not for me. I hate that green stuff. What else are we having?"

"Pot roast left over from last night, new potatoes, green beans."

"Leave me out on the green beans."

Chop went the knife. Chop. Chop.

"What the hell are you putting in that salad now? I can smell it from here."

"Spring onions," said his wife.

"You know I hate them."

"You're not going to eat them, so why do you care?"

"They smell like cat pee."

"I'll put the salad downwind," said his wife.

"Is that supposed to be a joke?"

"No," she said.

The pause settled. The knife chopped. The paper rattled.

"I know what I'll call them."

"The onions?"

"No, dummy. The dogs. How's this for a name? 'The Hounds of Hell.' Pretty good, huh?"

"If you think the neighbors' yard is hell."

"Sure looks like it most of the time."

"They're raising dogs, not flowers."

"They'd be pushing up the daisies if I had my way."

"Isn't that a little extreme? Besides, if their dogs are the hounds of hell, where does that leave you? When you go out the door you're at the mouth of hell."

"Very funny. You're killing me."

"I read a story," said his wife, slicing away, "about a dog at the mouth of hell. It . . ."

"Don't," said Geoffrey Fuller, "get started on your stories again. I couldn't care less. I'm sick and tired of you yapping about some fairy tale while I'm trying to read the soccer scores."

". . . barked every time a damned soul arrived."

"Yeah, well, any damn soul with two brain cells would just turn around and go home. You don't have to go to hell."

"Do you not?" said his wife.

She picked up a mushroom, laid it on the board, beheaded it neatly.

"I don't hear of many people who come back," she observed.

Holding the mushroom cap steady on the board, she plied her knife. A little row of slices marched to one side.

"Once you're there, you're stuck, I've always heard."

Done with the mushroom, she laid aside the knife, shoveled the vegetables into the salad bowl, and reached for the olive oil, but her hand shook, and a few drops spilled on the countertop. She left them there.

Outside, a chorus of yapping erupted.

"There they go again!" said her husband. "I'm damned if I'm going to listen to that racket all night."

He threw down his newspaper and rose to his feet. Swinging open the door, he bellowed into the night.

"Shut the hell up, you damn hounds!"

He stood silhouetted against the lamplight that spilled out into the night. Behind him, the latch clicked as the door quietly swung to, taking the light with it.

"I'll give you something to bark about!"

He took a menacing step forward.

Now the only light came from the eyes of the dogs, ranged in a half-circle and barking even louder. Geoffrey Fuller stood his ground. The dogs came no closer, but their eyes gleamed red, and they barked and barked.

"What the hell," he said to himself. "They're only dogs."

Only when he turned to go back inside did he make the discovery that his front door was shut, and only when he twisted the knob did he realize that it was also locked. In vain he rattled the knob and knocked and kicked and called and cursed, but no matter what he did, the door stayed shut, and the dark waited to swallow him, and the dogs went on barking barking barking.

Gavál and Dórvos

*T*wo *brothers, Gavál and Dórvos—one light, one dark—haunt each other as female animals. Dórvos is stalked by Gavál's soul, a golden-furred cat with amber eyes. Gavál is pursued by Dórvos' soul, a silver-winged hawk with eyes of tarnished silver. The souls take shape as women who lead the brothers to their deaths. In a final struggle when in their animal forms, the souls destroy each other. No one knows who it was who first told the story, least of all who wrote it down, and maybe they were the same, but it was Elly found the pages scattered in a pile of leaves raked up for burning and took them up one by one and took them home, and in the evenings when the chores were done she spelled them out word by word and page by page until she had as much as they could tell her. This is what she read.*

Once there were two brothers, Gavál and Dórvos. They lived in a village not far away, but so long ago that everything has changed since. The brothers were as alike and as different as two can be who have folded together in the same dark universe, floated against one another in the same warm ocean, fallen one after another through the same narrow passage into the cold light. As babies they nursed at the same breasts and fell asleep cradled in the same arms, but for all that, each lived a different life, for each had a brother who was not himself. As small boys they played and fought and ate and slept together, each taking for granted that the other was the necessary and immutable half of his world. They fitted together like the right hand and the left, sometimes clasped, sometimes opposite, but always matching. As they grew they began to look beyond their private horizon to a wider, more various universe that threatened their little kingdom with difference. Each went deeper into his own self. Each measured that self against the other and against the world. Each began to learn who he was and what he was about. And the differences between them widened. So it went on until they were men.

Gavál was sturdy of build, broad of shoulder, with golden skin and green-gold eyes with little shiny flecks like mica in them. He had broad cheekbones and a square mouth, mobile and quick to laughter. His hair, a darker gold than his skin, clung closely around his head, and the tendrils curled against the nape of his neck in a way that turned women's hearts to butter. He was well aware of the effect, enjoyed it, and often followed where it led, but never took unfair advantage. He was good at love, and stayed friends with his lovers when the love came to a close, as it always did. He had many friends, men and women. Everyone liked Gavál.

Gavál enjoyed his life, turning it in his hands like a shining ball, taking a sensuous pleasure in the gleaming surface. He was sunny and even-tempered, fond of songs and jokes, of good food and good company, and he laughed easily and often. From a boy he had worked with wood, whittling it, carving it, fashioning dolls and flutes for the children who clustered round him, finding grotesque humor in the faces he brought out of the twists and gnarls of tree-roots. He liked the clean feel of new-sawn wood under his hands and the clear smell of it in his nostrils. As a man he was skilled with saw and chisel, plane and drill, could turn you out an inlaid table for feasting, carve you a pair of fine chairs to furnish out a room, or run you up a smoothly joined chest of many drawers in which to store beautiful things.

Gavál lived in a house he had built himself on a busy corner where two streets met. The top floor was a large, sunny bedroom with an outside stair leading down to the woodyard. One corner of the yard overflowed with stacks of boards cut to different lengths and sizes; the rest was littered with chips and shavings, and soft underfoot with sawdust. In summer the night breeze brought to his window the sharp, clean smell of pine, the sour, milky smell of oak, the pungent sweetness of maple and cherry, and the deep, oily smell of walnut. The bottom floor, which gave out onto the yard, was both shop and workshop. The front half was fitted up with a counter for orders and a space for the finished pieces, smoothed and polished and set out for display. The back half was a cavernous jumble of works in various states of incompletion, for Gavál had a habit of working on several things at once, moving from one to another as the impulse took him.

If Gavál was gold, Dórvos was quicksilver, sudden and shifting in mood, lithe-limbed and quick in movement, spare of speech. His eyes were the changeable grey of storm clouds when the wind comes up, and his dark hair fell crookedly over one eye, like the broken wing of a bird, so that he had often to brush it aside or toss it back off his face. A hawk nose arched over the stubborn mouth that kept a narrow line of defense against what the world might think or say. He was quick to darken, unexpected to brighten, like the leaves of a forest that turn over all at once when the wind changes. What he learned he taught himself. He laughed not often, but when he did it was with his whole self, like a very young child. No one disliked Dórvos. But no one was especially drawn to him either, and so he walked by himself. He might have been lonely, if he had thought about it. But he did not think about it, and so he was sufficient and content.

He lived some distance from the town in a shack down by the river, and his skiff was drawn up in a little sandy place just below his door. Sometimes in the snowmelt and rains of spring the river came into the shack, and then Dórvos took his pallet and blanket and went to higher ground. When the river fell again, he came back. He could spend whole days on the water or wandering in the meadowlands that opened on either side of the river. Their empty spaces were not empty to him, but filled with the small hoppings and rustlings, the little chirps and creaks and high, distant calls of wild creatures who do not know that humans are listening. Dórvos liked stone, and he came up from the river or back from the dry plains with his pockets filled with stones of many shapes and hues, some rough and glittering with fool's gold, some smoothly polished by the wind or the river. His favorites were two satiny stones streaked brown and gold that he carried always in his pocket. So smooth that they were almost soft to the touch, they fitted together like two hands, and when he slid them one over the other they made a sound like crickets calling, or sleepy birds at evening. The sound was soothing when the world perturbed him, as it often did.

Dórvos knew stone, knew its many subtle shades of color, its textures, its hardness and yet its willingness to be shaped if only the shaper followed where it led. He could take a set of rounded, shining river-pebbles and string them into a necklace, or polish a single stone till it shimmered like a cat's eye, green or brown or honey-colored. His long, thin fingers caressed stone as softly as if it were silk or velvet. Most of the things that he made he gave away to anyone who asked for them, but a few, whose shape or color pleased him, he kept. Not many, though.

Dórvos was often wakeful at night. The slightest of noises—a twig snapping, an owl hooting, a rustling in the branches, a pebble clattering over stones—could call him out of restless sleep. As often as not there was no noise at all, and still he would come involuntarily out of sleep, and then he would lie awake, following his thoughts wherever they led him. This night, wide-eyed in the dark for what seemed hours, he at last drifted imperceptibly into an uneasy sleep haunted by unremembered dreams, and after one dream more disturbing than the rest, he became aware that he was awake again and that, although he could see nothing, he was not alone. Someone or something was in the room with him.

He sensed a presence, felt rather than heard soft footfalls approaching his pallet over the dirt floor, felt a breathing that ruffled his hair and carried a smell of autumn leaves. He lay still, acutely aware that he was being sniffed over from head to foot and back again. He heard a sound—like a cat purring, but bigger, louder than any cat he had ever known and so near and immediate that it seemed to be coming from inside his own head. It swelled to thunder, filling his mind, filling the corners of the room, taking possession of him until his world was nothing but sound. How long it lasted he could not tell. Then the purring stopped, and he heard soft footfalls padding out the open door. The room was empty, and he was alone again. Without hesitation he got up to follow.

Outside, cold moonlight lay over the world like silver gauze, and only steps from his door the river, a shining serpent, flowed in lazy coils. Nothing unexpected was in sight, but he felt or heard something moving up the slope away from the river. He turned and followed, and the shadow went before him, passing through the little town like an unbodied spirit and so away and out into the open land. It seemed he followed forever, walking as one does in dreams, without feeling the ground underfoot, with no sense of time passing. The moon climbed the black sky over his head, and he walked on and on. Ahead, on the encircling edge of the world, the mountains rose stark and abrupt out of the plain, their vales and ridges etched sharp in moonlight. Still moving timelessly he crossed the immense distance and found himself climbing the lower slopes dotted with groves of aspen and maple. As he ascended, the trees clustered thicker, surrounding him and bending a canopy of branches between him and the watching moon. The path was latticed with shadow where the branches crossed the moonlight. The trees swayed, though there was no wind, and the bars of shadow shifted and danced under his feet.

A little way ahead another shadow was moving, passing smoothly from dark to light to dark to light. The way wound up and up, twisting around great tree-trunks and skirting rocks dropped by a giant hand in some past age. It seemed he walked for hours, and the leafy forest gave way to towering, shaggy-boled pine and spruce, and the darkness deepened until the very air he breathed tasted thick and black. In one step Dórvos came out from deep shadow, and the moonlight struck him full in the face, taking his breath away. He was standing at the edge of a level clearing, the mountain's lap. On three sides the clearing was walled with the rough trunks of tall trees. The fourth side was open, and its edge was a precipice whose depth he could feel but not see that fell away in plunging dark straight to the valley floor. It was like a little outdoor room whose roof was black sky with the moon hanging just above his head like a lantern. The floor of the clearing was turf as short and smooth and close-cropped as a grazing meadow.

And in the center, playing with the moonlight, was a mountain cat, savage and golden-tawny, with pricked ears and tufted tail. All this way she had led him, and now she seemed unaware of his presence, wholly concentrated on her game with the moonlight. She was leaping and retreating, batting at the light with her paws, bounding in and out, dancing soft and lazy, as if the light caressed her. The air sounded with silent music. She stopped suddenly, and the music stopped, and he knew that she had seen him. Only the tip of her tail moved, swinging to and fro, to and fro, ever so slowly.

And then as he looked, her shape seemed to waver, as if a wind had touched it, and then it was a woman who held his gaze with amber eyes. She was motionless with the gathered, quivering tension of a waiting cat, but her tiger-tawny hair, echoing the dance, swung about her shoulders, and across her body the moonlight shimmered, rippling to and fro, to and fro, ever so softly, like a silk dress blowing in the wind.

"Who are you?" he asked, but his voice had no sound. "What do you want of me?"

It was only a moment, and then the light rippled again, and she was in her animal shape. For a long moment they stared at one another, cat and man, and then she padded deliberately toward him and rubbed against his leg. He put his hand on her head, and she pushed against it, as a beast will do when it wants attention. Her fur was thick and soft to his touch, and the feel of her body against his tugged at his memory. He felt unexpectedly, unforeseeably happy, as if he had been long searching for the thing he wanted most and had found it at last.

It was a feeling he had almost forgotten, half remembered from certain dreams he used to have when he was little, dreams wherein, though he could not remember their substance, everything was as it should be; there was unimaginable comfort and quiet certainty and joy, and everything came out right. He found that he had turned away from the little outdoor room, but he knew she was beside him, and in natural companionship they walked together back into the shadows and along the little gnarly path toward home. As he emerged out of the dark wood, the moonlight fell full on his face, and he pushed the covers away and sat upright in his bed with the morning sun coming in the window, and he was alone.

For an instant as excruciating as it was brief he felt his heart tear loose inside his rib cage, a wrenching agony that stopped his lungs breathing and drained his vital spirits. The breath left his body, and he saw his soul go with it, floating on the air like a mist. Then it was over. He drew in a long breath, but the mist did not come back. He felt a hunger for a thing he could not name.

All that week the weather varied between sunny and changeable, bringing an alternation of sudden, silvery showers and a sunlight so brilliant the newly washed world sparkled like cut glass. When Dórvos passed The Spotted Owl on his way to nowhere, the most recent shower had cleared, leaving puddles that mirrored the emerging stars. A waning moon, burnished by the wind that came off the mountain, contended with the red glow of the fire shining out the tavern door. Riding on the firelight, the fragrances of hot, strong coffee and burnt bread mingled with the thicker smells of stews simmering and onions sputtering in hot oil that scented the air. Dórvos paused in the roadway for a moment, feeling the light on his face and the dark at his back. He had a liking for such contradiction, and so he stood savoring the contrast. Then he saw Gavál seated at a table near the door.

Gavál was at a low wooden table just inside the open doorway. In front of him was a plate of thin-sliced beef dusted with pepper, and next to that a bowl of curly lettuce topped with chunks of fresh tomato, the whole dressed with oil and vinegar and a little garlic. There was a crusty half-loaf of new bread and beside it a little crock of very yellow butter. To make all perfect, a wooden board held a wedge of cheese, red gold and pungent, scenting the air with sharp fragrance. Gavál was devoting himself to each thing in its turn, sending down mouthfuls of beef with bites of lettuce and tomato, following these with large cuttings of bread and butter topped with generous hunks of cheese, washing it all down with great gulps of strong, steaming coffee. He glanced up to see Dórvos passing the open door, swallowed, and called out.

"Dórvos! Where have you been hiding? I haven't seen you since—well, in far too long. Come and have some coffee."

Dórvos hesitated, half shook his head, then shrugged and took the stool by the open door. Something in Gavál's voice rang oddly in his ear—a tone of suppressed excitement, of something hidden yet eager to be revealed. Folding himself down, he leaned back against the door-frame, his long legs stretched in front of him, ankles crossed. He took a pinch of the bread and rolled it in his slim fingers, tossing it idly from hand to hand. Though neither would say it, they were glad to see each other. Gavál fiddled his fingers on the table, looked out the doorway, looked back into the room, slanted troubled eyes at Dórvos, slanted them away again. He said nothing.

"I thought you wanted to talk," said Dórvos through a mouthful.

Gavál swung round on his stool, nearly toppling it. "A thing happened. Last night," he said.

Dórvos raised an eyebrow, mouth once more full of bread and cheese, but said nothing.

"It was so strange. I tell you, Dórvos, it was like—I don't know— And now—"

Dórvos waited.

Gavál took a deep breath, started over, speaking to no one, like a man in a troubled dream.

"Well, you know me, I don't usually have any trouble sleeping. I fall asleep before I'm under covers, and I'm dead till daylight. But not last night. Last night I couldn't sleep for anything. My shoulders hurt and my legs ached and my feet twitched. All night I was turning, one side and then the other, squirming and fidgeting. My legs got tangled in the blanket, and all the rest of me was cold. And when I put the blanket right, the pillow was bunched wrong. So I threw it on the floor, and I thought at last I would sleep, but a minute later my eyes opened by themselves.

"Then I sat straight up. I was listening for—I don't know what, something that faded as I caught it, the ghost of a sound. The moonlight was like a shaft coming in the window, and it picked out two bright spots on the door-hinge—nailheads or studs, I suppose. Perfectly ordinary, of course, but my eyes were playing tricks, and it looked like the bright spots were coming toward me, floating across the darkness. They got brighter and brighter, and the longer I looked the more they began to look like eyes coming closer. You know how an animal's eyes reflect the light? That funny glow? Only the moon was behind them, and there was no light to reflect. And I felt a wind, like wings beating, though the air outside was calm. It's strange, you know; I knew that a bird of prey was hovering over me, and yet I felt no fear."

"That was foolish," said Dórvos. "If it really was a bird of prey, it could have attacked you, torn your throat out."

"I didn't think of that. I don't suppose I thought at all, really. For a long moment—I don't know how long—nothing happened. As if everything was standing still. And then the eyes receded, and became just two bright spots on the door-hinge again. And the wind stopped.

Whatever it was, it was gone. So I got up and followed, down the stairs and out into the night. It was so still. And silent. Once I heard a night bird call, but that only made the silence deeper. And the light was so— Have you ever tried to follow anything in moonlight? It tricks your eyes so that the shadows change as you come near them, and the dark takes on peculiar shapes, shapes you'd never see in daylight. That's how it was.

"The shadows of the houses fell across the road like bars of darkness, and another shadow, her shadow, winged in and out of them as she went. She was coasting down toward the river, flying low and slow, as if to let me follow. It seemed to take forever. We left the houses behind. I could see the river ahead, see it plain, but I couldn't make any headway, couldn't come any closer to it. And I couldn't see her clearly, only shadows moving. I could smell the wet earth-smell of the mud-flats and the fresh green of the willows hanging over the water. And then we were at the river, and she disappeared. A big willow leaned out over the water, and I knew she had come to light on a branch over my head. I looked straight up, and she was silhouetted against the moon, wings folded. She was a silver kestrel, a windhawk. She was beautiful."

"How could you tell she was beautiful if you couldn't see her?" asked Dórvos. "And how do you know it was a she? You keep saying 'she,' 'her,' as if you knew. Why are you so sure?"

"That's exactly what is so strange," said Gavál. "I didn't see anything except a shadow, and yet within it I knew there was such beauty . . ." He hesitated, searching for words. "And I knew—knew—that whatever it was, whoever it was . . ."

Dórvos' eyebrow crept up again.

". . . was she. And I was right, for as I looked, she turned toward the moonlight, and I saw a face—a human face, with hair made of shadows and eyes the color of tarnished silver."

Dórvos raised an eyebrow.

"You're getting poetic, Gavál, and that's not like you."

"Don't joke, Dórvos; this is serious."

He leaned forward. "Now listen. We looked at each other, I don't know how long. Then the face turned away into the shadows, like a beast when you look in its eyes, and when it turned back it was a hawk's face again, wild and fierce. That was what I had been following. That was what came into my room. She must have come down from the mountains. But how she got into my room— Or why—"

He gave a wry laugh, but his eyes held bewilderment.

"I spoke to her. I did. I know that sounds absurd; you don't try to have conversation with a wild bird, but at the time it seemed perfectly natural, as things do in dreams, though this was no dream. I said, 'Who are you? What do you want of me?'"

Dórvos closed his eyes. In his left-hand pocket, cool in his fingers, were the two smooth stones, but only he could hear the little cricket-sound as he slid them one on another.

Gavál went on.

"Of course she didn't say anything, just stared at me, her eyes glowing like moonstones. 'Who are you?' I said again, but my words made no sound. And then she took flight, circling higher and higher till I thought she must touch the moon. And then without any warning she dived at me. Straight down, like a falcon stooping on its prey. Then I was afraid. Terrified—she came so sudden. I threw up my arm to ward her off, but she caught me on the shoulder and threw me off balance. As I fell I flung my arms out to keep her away, and she came straight into them, talons outstretched for the kill. I'm not a coward, Dórvos, you know that, but I shut my eyes. I couldn't help it. I knew it was my death, and there was nothing I could do. I felt her full weight, felt her wings spread above me like night, and then everything shifted, and it was a woman I held in my arms, fierce and tender. She was right on top of me."

He stopped, eyes shut. He was seeing other eyes shining inside his lids. The space where his voice had been filled with silence, slowly, as a forest pool fills with rain. At last Dórvos could bear it no more. "Well?" he said. "What happened?"

Gavál blinked, coming back from a precipice. "Nothing. When I opened my eyes a moment later, sunlight was streaming in the open door, and I was snuggled under the bed-cover with the pillow over my head. The room was empty. It was broad daylight, and no one was there but me."

For a while neither spoke. The silence floated between them, and they let it be, waiting to see who would break first.

"Well," said Dórvos at last.

"Well?" said Gavál.

"Well, what? We can't go on saying 'well' forever."

"Well, what do you make of all of it? I tell you about something so strange, so unlike anything that has ever happened to me before, and you sit there with that look on your face and all you say is 'well'?"

"What do you want me to say?"

"I don't know."

Gavál shook his head like a man coming up from deep water. "Who was she? Was she a woman or a bird? Do you think she was a dream? I can't believe she was; it all felt so real. I could touch her, feel her weight, smell her. I tell you, I knew her, Dórvos. And yet it must have been a dream, because she was gone; the tree was gone; the river was gone; and there I was in my bed in my room as if nothing had happened. But it had happened. I know it."

He shook his head once more in vague bewilderment, and brushed his hand across his eyes like a man brushing away cobwebs.

"It was real, wasn't it?" He looked at Dórvos, his face almost comic in its distress. "I wasn't dreaming, I'd swear it. There must be something—"

What is real? thought Dórvos. And what difference does it make? He drained his coffee in one gulp and stood up abruptly. Gavál stood as well, knocking over the stool. He righted it carefully, forked in a last mouthful of beef, flung some coins on the table, and followed Dórvos out the door.

They could have walked together, but they went their separate ways, each following his own road, each thinking about the other.

Exhaustion dropped on Dórvos like a cloak settling around his shoulders. It was sudden and total, pressing on his neck and making his eyes throb with fatigue. He flexed his shoulders and stretched his arms, trying to shake off the feeling, but it only clung more persistently around him. Ordinary tiredness he was used to—the good tiredness that came at the end of the day or a long tramp through the countryside, the satisfying ache of muscles stretched to their uttermost, limbs pleasantly heavy with the message that it was time for rest. This was another tiredness, a weight on his soul as well as his body, and yet with it a hollow feeling, as if his bones were filled with smoke.

A contrary wind gusting both ways at once met him as he turned the corner, spinning the new-fallen leaves around his feet and harrying them along the road ahead of him. To his tired imagination they seemed like puppies tumbling over one another, chasing their tails, scurrying frantically to go nowhere. Just ahead of him a swirl of them spiraled straight up, and he thought they were like a flight of birds that took to the air, circled for a space, and returned to earth as quickly, tired of the game. Their rustling echoed on the wind, and sounded like hurrying footsteps coming up behind him. He half turned, hopeful that it might be Gavál, but it was only the leaves skidding dry fingers over the stones.

As he turned back, a gust scooped up a double handful of leaves and flung them at his face. The flurry caught him unaware, momentarily blinding him with furious wings that beat against his eyes, then fell back to earth, dispersing as swiftly as they had attacked. In their mad whirl they took for a fleeting instant a coherent shape, like a woman running away from him up the deserted street, and he had a momentary vision of long hair flying out like wings on the wind. Then the vision died, and there were only the leaves scuttering restlessly ahead of him, leading him home.

To Gavál's weary legs the stair up from the woodyard seemed to climb forever, and every separate step dragged at his feet. When at last he gained the top and pushed open the door to his room, he was staggering with weariness. Without bothering to undress he dropped onto his bed and fell headlong through the pillow into a waking dream that circled endlessly through his mind like birds flying, flying. One bird, larger than the rest, broke away from the flight and swung back to ride the air over his head, balancing lower and lower until he could see her face bending just above him, her lips half open, her dark hair brushing his face like the shadows of wings. Her eyes gathered the light of the setting moon, and as he looked deep into them they seemed to him like stars drowning in a forest pool. He reached his arms to her, and she came into them as softly as sleep, and the stars dissolved into darkness.

That's all there is except a letter or two is missing here and there on some ragged edge where the leaves have been ripped out of a book. How does the story end? You must follow it through according to your own desire.

Outside

They brought her home from the shelter in a box with a door that they opened so she could explore her new surroundings. There were no other cats around, but after the shelter with its narrow cages everything seemed very big and full of things, and it took her a while to get used to all the different spaces.

They named her Ginger after the color of her fur, which was the golden brown of a gingersnap cookie. They gave her one to sample, but the spice bit her tongue, and she spat it out and shot them a look that said, 'Don't try that again.' So they gave her cat kibbles instead and scratched her behind the ears and brushed her fur to keep it fluffy. That was much better, and so for a while all went well. The apartment was on the second floor of a tall house, up a flight of stairs and with windows that looked out into the treetops. They kept her inside for fear, as they told her, that if she got outside, she would get lost. But they allowed her to sit in the big chair by the upstairs window and see the outside from the inside.

She saw the birds fly back and forth on unknown errands and weave their nests and hatch their young in the branches of the maple tree that brushed its leaves against the panes of her window. She saw the fledglings learn to fly and leave the nests to build on their own. She watched the squirrels chase each other up and down and round and round the trunk. She saw them pile leaves for sleeping places way up where the branches forked, so they could look out on the world from a perch even higher than the birds.

Sometimes the window was open, and the breeze came through the screen and stirred her whiskers. Other times the window was shut, and rain fell, and drops ran down the panes. Sometimes the leaves on the tree turned red and yellow and wind chased them about and danced them against the window in flurries that tapped against the glass. Sometimes white snow came soft and silent from the air to pile up on the tree branches and gather on the windowsill and make the window cold where her nose pressed against it. The snow would lie there for a while, and then it would go away, and presently the leaves would turn green once more. This happened so regularly that Ginger came to expect it. That was the way things were in the world outside. There was a lot of outside to see, and so for a while she was content.

But after a while Ginger wanted more. She wanted to smell and hear and feel for herself all the things she saw through the window, the things that belonged to outside. If you want a thing sure enough and long enough and hard enough, it will happen. Ginger kept on wanting, knowing that her time would come, and so it did. One day the door stood open, and no one was around. Ginger seized her moment. She jumped down from the chair, and before they could come, she ran out and down the stairs so quickly and quietly that they never heard or saw. At the foot of the stairs there was another door, and it was open too, so she took her chance and slipped through that door as well. She found herself on a cement platform only a little larger than her chair, with railings on the sides and green shrubbery beyond the railings.

'So this is outside,' she said to herself. Outside was different at ground level from what she saw through the window. It was bigger and colder and not nearly as inviting. The tree trunk rose like a tower straight and tall, and the branches loomed over her head, so far above she could hardly see them, while the birds were just dark moving patches against the bright sky. The rough cement of the platform rasped the pads of her paws, and the harsh smell of the street stung the inside of her nose, and the shissing sound and loud blare of the cars in the roadway hurt her ears.

'Nevertheless, ' she told herself as she surveyed the territory, 'I'm here now, so I might as well make the most of it. I'll just take a quick look around, and then I'll go back to my chair where it's warm and quiet.'

That was when she heard the click. She whirled to see that the downstairs door had swung to behind her, shutting her out just when she thought about going back in.

She scratched with her paw, but the door did not respond. She knew, of course, that sooner or later they would see she was gone and come looking for her. They would pick her up and carry her inside and put her back on her chair where she belonged. So she waited patiently, but sooner turned into later, and none of that happened. Time went by, and no one came, and the door stayed shut.

'Rats!' said Ginger to herself. 'What am I going to do now?'

"What are you going to do now?" said a voice.

She looked up to see a squirrel sitting on a branch above her head, his tail curved into a plume behind him. He was nibbling an acorn and scattering the broken bits on her head.

"You've done it now," he told her with doleful relish. "That door won't open by itself. You're well and truly stuck."

That was too obvious to require comment.

"You might as well enjoy your freedom while you've got the chance," he remarked. "Why don't you explore those bushes?"

For all her curiosity she hadn't thought of that, especially since she hadn't known the bushes were there, but she took his suggestion and slipped down among the leafy brambles that flanked the cement stoop. Here the world was different yet again. It was dark and damp and prickly, smelling of growth and moist earth, but not nearly as nice as her chair, and even colder than the stoop. The brambles caught at her tail and tugged at her fur whenever she tried to move, so she tried not to move. That made it easy for the cold to creep under her skin and settle in her bones.

She started to shiver.

Ginger began to regret her hasty impulse. It occurred to her, but too late, that perhaps Outside was not as good a place for a cat as she had thought.

A sudden loud shout made her jump, and her jump made the brambles scratch her even more.

"What was that?" she asked the squirrel.

"A dog barking," he told her, but that was no help as she didn't know what barking was, let alone a dog. She found out soon enough.

A large snout poked through the bramble, sniffing as it came. The rest of the dog pushed into her hideout, big and shaggy and with a pungent new smell that she didn't like at all. Without thinking, she took a swipe with her paw. The dog backed away, and Ginger burst through the brambles into daylight where she skidded to a halt and found herself nose to nose with the dog. What happened next surprised her as much as the dog.

A shudder rippled through her fur, her back arched, and every single hair on her body spiked and stood on end. A reaching, screeching yowl came out of her throat, and there came an ominous answering growl from the throat of the dog.

"Up here!" called the squirrel, and she made a dash for the tree and was halfway up the trunk before she was aware of what she was doing. When that dawned on her, she was too scared to climb higher, but it was too late to back down, so she clung where she was, legs spread, claws out and clutching.

"Up! Up!" urged the squirrel. "You can't stay there!"

"There's nowhere else to go," said Ginger. "I really am stuck."

Below her the dog was standing at full stretch on its hind legs but still unable to reach her. The heavy gusts of its panting breath blew against her tail like the wind that chased the leaves. She hung suspended between sky and earth.

"Push and pull!" called the squirrel. "Push and pull. You can do it!"

It was impossible. She had never done it.

She did it.

She pushed and pulled and jerked herself upward in convulsive bursts, each one the last until the next and then the next, and then she was up and dragging herself out along the branch to lie panting with her tongue hanging out.

"Good job," said the squirrel.

For a long time she did nothing but breathe, but that was enough. After a while she looked up and looked around her.

"Is it always like this?" she asked the squirrel. "Outside?"

"Pretty much," said the squirrel. "You'll get used to it."

That was when the door opened, and they came out.

"There she is!"

"Where?"

"Up in the tree. See there? On that branch. Heeere Ginger! Come on, girl. Giiinger, come daaown."

'Never' vowed Ginger to herself. 'They can call all they want, but I am never ever leaving this tree. Certainly not while that dog is there.'

But the dog was not there. Defeated by the tree, it had lost interest and wandered off in search of easier prey.

Ginger looked down. The ground seemed a long way off. They looked so odd standing beneath the tree and holding up their hands, but her branch was beyond their reach.

'If the dog couldn't reach me,' she thought, 'they probably can't either. But I can't climb down this tree; it was hard enough getting up.'

"How do you manage?" she asked the squirrel. "It looks easy when you do it, but I'm not a squirrel."

"Put your head down," said the squirrel, "and go one paw at a time."

"I'll fall," said Ginger.

"It's the only way," said the squirrel.

In the meantime, they were still standing under the tree holding their hands out, reaching up to her.

"Come on come on come on," they coaxed.

She crept unsteadily along the branch, her claws alternately slipping and catching hold.

"That's it. Gooood girl."

She reached one paw down the trunk. Another paw. And another but then she lost her grip and went headfirst slithering and sliding, and they caught her halfway.

They bore her back in triumph through the door and up the stairs and safely inside with all doors closed. They rewarded her with kibbles, but no one was entirely comfortable until she jumped up into her chair, turned twice around, and tucked her tail beside her paws.

"Don't try that again," they told her.

'No way,' she promised herself, but then, 'well . . . maybe I'll try tomorrow.'

And she did. But that is another story.

Tall Grass

Did I say it was a bad life? You're not listening.

You better start paying attention, youngster, before you go asking any more questions. Curiosity? Go on! Curiosity's no excuse for the pestering you put a body through. I've had a long day, and I could use a little peace and quiet now it's over. There's such a thing as good manners, you know. Or don't you?

Well now, that's better. Apology accepted. Nothing wrong with being polite to your elders. Glad to see you've learned that much, anyway.

Well, of course I know more than you do. Ought to—after all this time. But if you think I know so much, you'd do well to keep your mouth shut and your ears open. Ask fewer questions, you'll get more answers.

Is that a promise? All right then, here's a start—and straight from the horse's mouth, as the saying goes.

First thing you need to learn is tolerance. My way of thinking: there's no better place to learn tolerance than a dude ranch. Dealing with the public needs more patience than most folks are born with. And dudes—well, they're a special segment of the public. Some of the things they do—you don't want to hurt their feelings, but it's hard to keep from laughing. Between a horse and a dude, I'll take the horse any day. The dumbest horse I know is smarter than the smartest dude.

Stands to reason. You've heard the expression "horse sense"? That's not just a figure of speech. It's based on observation. A good horse, now; he knows what to do better than his rider, nine times out of ten. A horse'll just naturally watch where he's going, where a dude'll be gawping at the scenery and walk right into a gopher hole from paying no mind to where he puts his feet. City people, the whole herd of them, though now and again you do get one knows which end of the horse is the front.

Come right down to it, it's not the dudes that put the most strain on your patience, dang fools though most of them are. Nossir. My way of thinking: the hardest thing to put up with is being bossed around all the livelong day.

"Do this. Now do that. No, don't do it this way, do it that way. The customer is always right."

Made me feel downright unappreciated when I first got here. Been making my own way in the world ever since my mama died, and I didn't take kindly to being told what to do by people not half as smart as me—and that's most of 'em. I like being my own boss, and I didn't welcome being everlastingly ordered around. Believe you me, sonny, there were some powerful contentions, what you might call "differences of opinion," before I concluded it was easier to cooperate than to argue.

That's what I mean by tolerance. Darn right it doesn't come easy. That's what I'm trying to tell you.

You young folks think life is a game. Racing hell-for-leather over the high plains with the wind in your hair and the wide-open spaces for your playground. Far as you're concerned that's all there is to it. Well, I'm here to tell you, my young friend, this life is not all it's cracked up to be. Take it from me, son: it's no game. Not by a long gallop. Mostly it's work: hard, dull work and lots of it, as you'll find out before you're much older.

No, of course not all the time. Nothing's "all the time." Stands to reason. Bound to be *some* patches of excitement in any life. If it lasts long enough. Times when maybe you do race hell-for-leather with the wind in your hair. Though when that wind is straight off the high peaks with an edge like broken ice and what's in your hair is freezing rain and sleet, well, that's not a kind of excitement I hanker for. It all adds up at the end of the day, I guess, but the big moments, good or bad, are pretty scarce, let me tell you. What there's more of is those long dull stretches when nothing special seems to happen, and you just keep doing the same thing over and over. Right like you're told. It gets old pretty fast, I can tell you.

Just an expression. Means it happens so often and so regular there's nothing new about it. Maybe "boring" 's a better word than "old." Or even "dull." How 'bout "monotonous"? "Mind-numbing"? That make it clear?

Once you get used to it, a job's a job. Way I see it, they're all pretty much the same, and they're all tedious. As jobs go, this one here's tolerable, as you'll learn before you're much older. The food's good and regular, and the working conditions aren't so terrible—compared with other situations I've been in. Yes, you have to put up with a lot, but you also get an education in how to handle different kinds of folks. These ones here, they think they've got me broke, in a manner of speaking, and I'm content to let them suppose so. Saves a power of trouble in the long run.

Leave? Sure I could. Of course. Any time I wanted to. I know my way around the world, and I'm just naturally independent by temperament; always have been, ever since I was little. Had to be. My dad—now there was one tough old tyrant. He was King of the Herd and no doubt about it. You know how a stallion will take against his own sons when they start to get their growth? That's how he was, and that meant he come down hard on all us guys. He was okay with the young ones. Long as they were dependent and looked up to him, things were fine. But once they got bigger, started thinking for themselves, that was it. He just couldn't tolerate anyone likely to turn out as big as he was, so he'd drive them out one by one. They'd hang around home for a while, till he let them know in no uncertain terms they were no longer welcome, then they'd soon took off on their own. Not much choice, seeing what he was like.

Result was, coming along last like I did, I hardly knew any of my brothers. Wish I had, now it's too late. I guess my mama was sorry at losing her other sons—once gone they never came back—and I was the last and the baby and she made me her pet. But even as a little guy I was no mama's boy, not in my own opinion, anyway. I always liked better to be off by myself. So every chance I got I'd scat to the tall grass, as the saying is, just to look around, see what was there. That used to drive her crazy. She'd come after me at a fast trot.

Where you been? Why can't you stay put where I can find you?

She'd scoot me back to home ground before I knew what was happening. Now, that's all well and good when you're a kid, but when you're getting your growth . . . well, the time come when I lost patience with her everlasting nagging every time I wanted to be out on my own. At that age, of course, you don't have a big stock of patience to begin with, and you sure don't have any idea what being on your own really means. I soon found that out.

The hard way, of course. Only way to learn anything worth knowing. Just you remember that.

I was right about the age you are now when everything changed. She up and died on me.

No, she wasn't took sick. It wasn't anything I expected. I was out on my own one day, away up in the high meadow, not doing anything in particular, and she come running up to get me. And just when she come up, one of those spring snowstorms you get up in the high country caught us both by surprise. Bright sunny morning and then *whoosh!* all of a sudden sky goes dark and up comes the wind and right behind it snow and before you know it you're in the middle of a blizzard. It was what folks in those parts call an easterner, and they're the worst. Out there they come up so fast, those storms—time you can see one coming it's already too late to run.

We tried to run from that one, but we couldn't make it. I remember how scared I was and how we finally had to stop running because the snow was coming so fast we couldn't see through it. I was shuddering cold and didn't know whichaway to go, so I squeezed myself up against her for the only shelter there was. Only thing I knew to do. I trusted she'd keep me warm, and she did her best. Kind of leaned herself against me on the windy side, made herself a shelter against the snow that was freezing onto us as fast as it landed.

That was one bad storm all right. Well, I should say. Worst in my memory. Don't ask me how I managed to get through it. Looking back now I couldn't tell you for the life of me. Dumb luck, I guess, as much as anything else.

No, I couldn't tell you how long it lasted. I wasn't counting time. Everlasting's how it seemed. But when the wind finally stopped and the snow died down and the storm was over, I opened my eyes and looked at my mama. Her eyes were wide open too. Only they were covered with ice.

Froze to death.

I couldn't believe it. Of course, I didn't want to believe it, and I kept waiting for her to blink her eyes and show me she knew I was there. I wanted so bad for her to look at me, but she never did, just kept staring wide-eyed into that ice. Well, I didn't know what to do. I'd start to go away, and then come back, go away and come back. Hoping, you see. But her eyes never once moved, and finally I gave it up. That was the worst time of all. Talk about lost. I felt so forlorn I didn't know which way was up. I didn't ever want to go home, even supposing I knew anymore which direction it was or how to get there. She was all the home I had, and she was gone. Nothing left but snow and more snow, all windblown and drifted so every landmark I knew was buried, and I couldn't tell where I was or which way to go.

That's what can happen to you out there if you're not careful. Or even if you are. Just you remember that too, while you're at it.

Well, there I was, on my own. Just like my brothers, only I hadn't been drove away, just froze out, so to speak. Younger than they were, too, and I hadn't a notion how to get along. But you do what you have to and I was bound and determined I'd make it through somehow. I looked around for something to go by, but every which way I looked, all there was was white. I had to go somewheres, so I just started moving out, random-like.

Talk about lonesome. That was it, mister. All I could tell, I was the only creature in the whole wide world. I kicked around in a lot of places up there, and in all that time I did not see one single solitary other individual. Lonesome days and lonesome nights. Nothing but the stars for company, and them so far away. Couldn't even tell time passing excepting how the moon changed. Now that I had all the freedom I wanted, it was anything but fun. All by myself not by choice but from necessity. At that point, I hankered to be my mama's baby, for sure. I'd have given anything then to have her back, nagging and all. She could have run after me day and night, and I wouldn't have minded. Nosiree. Spoiled rotten, my old dad used to say. He was probably right.

About when I was getting desperate, the weather took a change for the better, and life changed with it. Things eased up considerable, and I started to think maybe life was worth living after all.

I was moseying along, minding my own business and going nowheres, when I come around a bend and ran smack into a gang of young fellows just about my age larking around in the tall grass, cutting moonshines. Romping and fooling the way youngsters will, racing each other, play-fighting: a bunch of spring colts out from under their mothers' eyes, just enjoying their freedom.

When they spotted me, they stopped their fooling and sauntered up kind of casual-like to look me over. That looked promising. It was the first time since my mama died that I'd seen anybody that wasn't me, so I was eager to look them over, too. Too eager. Walked right up to them like a durn fool, expecting to be friends. Thinking they'd be like my brothers.

No such of a thing.

They weren't a bit like my brothers, and they soon let me know it. More like my father, truth be told, for they weren't what you'd call a friendly bunch. Just the opposite. Instead of a welcome I got insults, challenges, kicks—my, but they could kick! One of them even bit me, if you can believe it. Before I knew what was happening, it turned into a real fight, the first one I ever had, though not the last. Well, I might've been young, but I wasn't stupid, and it didn't take me long to figure they were bigger than me and I was out of my class. I backed off quick.

But I was so lonesome I couldn't help tagging behind, just for company. So I hung back a bit, the way young ones will, standing away, not quite with them, you understand, but always keeping them in sight.

They may have been bigger, but I wasn't mama's baby anymore, so soon enough I tried coming up to them again. No better luck than last time. Same old thing—kicks, yells, insults. No point arguing. Some folks are like that. I dropped back to my safe distance. But I kept them well in view. Now I'd found company I wasn't about to lose it, mean though they were. I did notice one little brown-haired runty fellow. Not much bigger than me, but curious-like. Not as bad as the rest. He kept looking at me sideways. Well, I'd show up, different times, different places, and finally, after I'd done it enough times, he dropped back a ways and we started talking.

Who are you? he says, looking at me like I was something he'd come across in the tall brush. It made me nervous.

Name's Buck, I says. *Short for Bucking Bronc, my mama used to say. Who are you?*

I'm Shorty, he tells me. *Not short for anything.*

It'll do, I says. *Fits the way you look.*

Where you from? he asks me.

Nowheres, I says. *Yonder. Up that way.*

Seen you following, he told me. *Where's the rest of your outfit?*

Got no outfit. Been on my own for a while now.

Why you following us the way you do?

Well, I'm hungry. And your bunch seems to eat pretty regular.

Food's easy enough to find if you know where to look.

He showed me where to look. Pretty soon him and me got to be buddies. When his gang kicked out at me for getting too close or made fun of him for cozying up to a stranger, why, he sided with me against them. So after a while, we turned our backs to them and struck out on our own. Buck and Shorty. Pardners. We got along good, a couple of youngsters on the loose—running wild with no tether. I loved the life we led then—roving where we wanted, standing up in the high hills looking out over the world, roaming the plains with the wind in our faces and the wide-open spaces for our playground. We could stop when we felt like it, sleep out wherever we wanted, follow our own time. We were beholden to no one but ourselves. It was like my early days, only without my mama coming up behind to chase me home.

I figured I was pretty smart, making it as far as I did without any help, but compared to Shorty, boy, I was nothing but a spring colt. Didn't know tall grass from tumbleweed, as the saying goes. Being a mite older'n me, he well knew how to get along. Smart as paint, he was. Knew how to keep away from official-looking busybody types trying to catch you up and socialize you, put their brand on you so to speak. Shorty knew out-of-the-way places to eat, when to run and where to hide and how to bed down where nobody would find us. I wouldn't of got far without him. Shorty and me, we each of us could tell what the other wanted by just a look in the eye or the tilt of a head.

That was the good time.

No, of course it didn't last. What do you think I'm doing here?

Well, I'm telling you, ain't I? If you'll just keep quiet for a change.

It's an inneresting story and a good lesson in what not to do, but we learned it just a little too late, the way you do most things. We were drifting along one day, minding our own business, going nowhere. Enjoying ourselves. Trouble was, we were having such a good time we forgot to keep a lookout. First thing we knew, here come a bunch of guys sneaking up. I didn't spot them until they were right up on us, but as soon as I did, I knew they were trouble. I didn't like their looks, and I didn't like their attitude, and I took against them yelling at us and crowding on us like we were a couple of dumb cows broke through the fence. So I look at Shorty and he looks at me, and he give a little wink, and I give one back, and we turn and high-tail it out of there as fast as we can, lighting out for the tall grass, as my mama would say.

We never even noticed the truck.

We were traveling fast, but those guys were mounted and traveling just as fast, and there were more of them than us, and pretty soon they had us surrounded. Well, it seemed like they had a plan, and it seemed like we were it. They were out looking to round up some additions to the workforce, and we were just the kind of range bums they had in mind: likely-looking, able-bodied drifters with no particular ambition and no fixed address. It's a bad way to hire anyone, if you ask me. But nobody asked me. We tried all our tricks—dodged, doubled, back-tracked, went in circles—but before we knew what was happening, we found ourselves in a corner with our backsides jammed up against a high fence. There we were, and there they were, and that was the end of fun and games.

Well, you hear about things like that. Everybody knows they happen to somebody else, but you don't never think it's going to happen to you. It does, though. Before you know it. Quicker'n a spring storm.

This next part gets kind of hazy, I'm afraid. Things were moving so fast I don't rightly recollect what-all happened next, except somewhere in there I got a knock on the head like to send me spinning, and after that there's some parts is just a blank. Last thing I recall was hearing a kind of loud *cr-e-e-e-a-k* like tree branches rubbing together in the wind, and then a real sharp *cleckk!*—like two rocks hitting. I look up, and danged if they haven't gone and penned us in like we was steers at a beef auction.

Get out? Well, what do you think? Of course we tried.

We took and ran against that fence and slammed into it full tilt. We were bound we'd bust it down or break through it, but they'd built it sturdy, and it stood fast. So when that didn't work, we turned around and lit into those guys hard as we could. I hit and kicked with everything I had in me, and Shorty he did too. Between us, we did our best to make a lasting impression on our new associates. We did manage to put several of 'em out of commission, broke a couple of heads, stove in some ribs. But there was more of them than there was of us, and in the end numbers prevailed. We were wasting our time and wasting our strength, and they just let us keep on till we plumb wore ourselves out.

When they figured we were finally too tuckered to have any fight left, they ushered us right into the truck. Hadn't noticed it before, but now it was all we could see—the back end open and waiting. Before we knew what was happening, they hustled us up a kind of ramp, slammed the door on us, and took off lickety-split. Boy, let me tell you: that was one rough ride, that old truck rocking and bouncing over the gopher holes and bucking like a bull in a rodeo. Too dark to see much of the inside, but I got acquainted with it in a highly personal way, skidding around and banging up against the side walls trying to figure out what in tarnation was going on. I'll remember every inch of that truck to my dying day.

There's a word for that kind of operation. "Hijacking." You just better hope it never happens to you.

Just about when we decided it was going to go on forever, the truck stopped, and next thing we knew we were being unloaded. Sun so bright it hurt your eyes. We were hot, tired, sore, and dirty. And confused. So Shorty, he says to me, *When you can't win, you might just as well lose*, and that's what we agreed to do. Besides, we were so dead beat by that time we practically fell asleep on our legs right where we stood, so battered we couldn't manage any more than keep upright. But that wasn't the end of the deal, not by a long shot. Then we got introduced to a whole new bunch. They looked us over, sized us up, decided we'd do. They were a different breed: a lot more civil than those first guys, I'll give them that. Seems like the others were just the middlemen between us and what turned out to be our new employers.

The circumstances began to look tolerable, at least in comparison to what we'd been experiencing.

Over the next week or so, we began to get acquainted with our new situation. Gradually. Met some other fellows been there a while, longer than us anyways, and they told us what the deal was. A ranch, only they didn't herd cattle, just people. We had to learn a whole new way of thinking, a whole new set of terms: "Dude." "String." "Trail." "In line." We didn't know what any of it meant, but they explained the procedure, told us it wasn't so bad once you got used to it. Well, Shorty and me, we didn't figure on getting used to it, both of us thinking, "Sooner or later we'll see our opening and light out for the tall grass when no one's looking." Not a chance, buster. They weren't ever not looking. They kept us new recruits on such a short rein you couldn't hardly get your head up to see around. I tried, though.

There was one bad incident. When I say "bad," I mean <u>bad</u>. I almost killed a guy. Not my fault I didn't succeed, either.

As I may have mentioned, I've never taken kindly to being shoved around. I've since learned tolerance, but in those days I was more inclined to put up a fight, thinking: *I don't have to take this, and they can't make me.* There was this one fellow. Smart-alecky. Thought he knew it all. Pushy, if you know what I mean. Him and me got off on the wrong foot with each other right from the get-go. He started in being bossy, and I right away adopted a policy of non-cooperation. That made him mad, and he got rough. And that made me mad, and I got rougher. It wasn't long before the state of affairs between us deteriorated into a flat-out battle of wills.

I've got a mean temper when I'm riled, just like my dad, and this guy, he had a mean temper too. The situation began to get ugly. I could feel the others watching, waiting to see who'd come out on top. I was bigger than him by a long sight, and I knew if I was drove too far, I could tromp him into little pieces. One fine day he drove me just a little too far, and that's exactly what happened. Or almost happened. He used his fist on me, and I went kind of crazy and took out after him with everything I had. Backed him into a stall in the barn and come close to ending the argument forever, only some other fellows heard the ruckus and come a-running. Jumped on me from both sides and dragged me off him before there was any serious damage.

I left my footprint on him, that's for sure. He's got it to this day.

In the long run, though, it didn't make any difference, and it didn't do me a bit of good. Only thing I got out of it was the silent treatment. Like being pushed out of the herd. I got stuck off by myself for a couple of days and kept on short rations to cool me down. I was pretty het up, so cooling down wasn't a short process. Worst part of it, though, was being kept away from Shorty. No one for me to complain to about unfair treatment. Shorty, every time he'd catch sight of me, he'd just shake his head, much as to say, *You ain't going to get anywheres kicking up a fuss. Live and learn, brother. Live and learn.*

Which is what he did. His way was always to work around things, put up with what he couldn't change and bide his time until he could. After a bit, I started to see some sense in that, especially since my way was only getting me in more trouble. So I decided to cooperate or at least make it seem like I was cooperating. Things got better. Meantime, we bided our time, him and me, kept our eyes open, started to catch on to the way things worked. We did eat regular, I'll say that. Most of the time. And it's easy to get used to eating regular, especially when you've been hungry to give you a taste of the difference. You can even get to like it if you don't watch out.

Well, from then on, it was just a matter of on-the-job training. Nothing but work work work till we were ready to drop in our tracks. We was rode hard and put away wet, as the saying is. Day after day after day, until we got it right. And when we did get it right, why then we had to do it all over again. And in spite of ourselves, we did get used to it. Matter of fact we got so used to it—seeing those dudes come sashaying down to the corral in their brand new hats and fancy-stitched boots and their chaps with the fringe, all ready to ride out into the sagebrush and play cowboys—we'd roll our eyes at each other, thinking: "Here's another bunch of greenhorns we got to educate."

It's just routine. Once you get the hang of it, you can do it with your eyes closed.

No, of course not really closed. Use your gumption, youngster. That's just an expression. Means it's so simple you don't have to pay attention.

You ride out every morning with a string of tenderfoots who don't know one end of a horse from the other. You learn to put up with fools, learn to take care of them when they get themselves in trouble—you wouldn't believe how easy they can fall off a horse, even at a walk. It takes patience and plenty of it, teaching them the right way to do things, making them feel good when they finally catch on. And just about the time you've got them broke in so they know to keep one leg on each side and their mind in the middle, why, that's when they up and leave. And then the next batch comes in and you got to start the whole business over again from scratch. It's enough to try the patience of a saint. If there is such a thing on a dude ranch. Which I doubt. Considering some of the types I've had to put up with.

Shorty? Sure, he's still around. That's the one good thing in the whole business. No matter where we are, we've stuck together all this time.

Oh, a pretty long time.

Come right down to it, I'm not sure I know exactly how long it's been. Long enough for me to see Shorty's hair turn frosty, like the muzzle of an old dog, and that's pretty long, seeing how young we were when we first came. My hair, too, if what I see on him is anything to go by. We bunk next to each other, see each other every day. We're still pals like we've always been. Keep together much as possible and try to work things so we go out with the same string if we can, so as to have some intelligent company. But we can't always manage it.

Shorty, he's good with the little ones. Tolerant. A way sight better than I am, that's for sure. Kids get on my nerves, all that yelling and screaming and bouncing around, and I'm inclined to lose my temper just a little bit if they don't behave. But being kind is just Shorty's nature. I guess it goes back to that first day when he dropped back out of his gang to talk to me. Whatever it is about him, they know to give him the littlest ones to train. Sometimes, when I'm out with a string, I can see him up on the ridge, going along slow and steady, keeping an eye on kids so little their legs stick out from the horse's back sideways and their feet can't hardly reach the stirrups. But he's there making sure everyone stays in the saddle.

Of course I miss being on my own, living the life I like. You never get over that.

Yes, indeed I think about it. Most every day. Especially mornings, when the breeze brings that spicy smell off the open range, or the wind carries a whiff of snow from off the high peaks. I can taste it like it was food.

Me and Shorty, we still talk about heading out, making for the tall grass. Evenings after the day's work is done, we put our heads together over chow, telling each other how we'll do it.

One of these days, soon as we get half a chance, we'll break out of here, head up into the high hills. Plenty of places to hide out up there. They'll never find us.

But lately . . . I don't know. I'm not so sure any more. Maybe I've just lost touch with that old life. Maybe it's too late. I don't know if we could manage like we used to, get the same kick out of being independent the way we did then. I don't know where the time goes. Just a little while ago we were spring colts feeling our oats and rarin' to go. Seemed like we could run all day and never get tired. And now it's all we can manage just to make it through from morning till evening. Couple of old-timers, the pair of us. Getting old pretty fast.

It's not such a bad life here. You can get used to anything after a while.

Oh, yes, you can, Mister Curiosity. What do you think I've been trying to tell you all this time? Never mind. You'll get it through your head one of these days, the way the world works. You and all the rest of the young ones.

And while I'm at it, here's another thing you can get through your head. You're not the only one around here's hungry when dinnertime comes. I've had a busy day and if you can't tell, I'm running short on tolerance. So if you'd be so kind as to take your nose out of that pile of hay and leave some for your elders, I need to get myself a bite to eat before I settle down for the night.

Tomorrow's another day.